GRANDMA'S PRECIOUS CHEST

Norah Kersh
Outback Series

Published by Boolarong Press, 35 Hamilton Road, Moorooka, QLD, Australia 4105

© **Norah V Kersh 2004**

(07) 4741 8708

National Library of Australia

Kersh, Norah

Grandma's Precious Chest

ISBN: 0 8643 9213 3

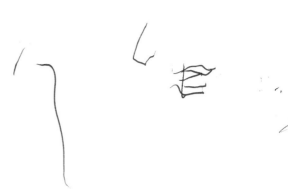

Dedication

To those who came from distant lands.
To the original Australians who worked
together through sunshine and showers
to create rainbows.

Acknowledgements

My grateful thanks to
Lyn Kersh who first read this stroy and encouraged me on.
My sister Fran Spora who helped me get my tense right.
Bob Marshall for allowing the use of his poem "Bringing up the Tail".
Marie Mahood friend and neighbour of Kimberley Territory days.
Tatum and all my family who continue to be my inspiration.

Tatum scrambled over stacked boxes, searching.

Tears ran down her cheeks.

In the corner were large plastic bags full of winter woollies and doonas. Under the window, boxes of linen, sewing machine, a jigsaw puzzle, an ironing board. Big boxes. Small boxes. Pots and pans.

Tatum and her family had just moved to Bora Station.

"Mummy, I can't find Teddy. I need Teddy!"

"I think I packed him in Grandma's precious chest" said Mum.

Tatum and her mother undid ropes and peeled off blankets packed around the precious chest.

There in the bottom drawer, was Teddy.

"Why do you call it Grandma's precious chest?" asked Tatum as she cuddled her Teddy.

"Lie on this pillow, Tate, and I will tell you", Mum replied, pulling a blue pillow from a bag.

"Now this is the story of Grandma Ruby and her chest of drawers".

In a small town in the Gulf country lived a little girl called Ruby. Her father's name was Ah Chee.

Many years before, Ah Chee had come from China, to dig for gold on the wild Palmer River.

One day he struck a very rich vein of gold.

Ah Chee sent a letter to his wife in China, with some gold for her passage to Australia.

Ruby's father and mother started a store near the river, and people came from near and far to buy supplies, groceries, fencing wire, swags and saddles, boots and hats, laces and ribbons. Ah Chee's store had it all, neatly stacked on wooden shelves, or in a tin shed out the back.

Ruby's family lived in a house on stilts by the store.

The window had sunshades with scalloped patterns cut out of tin.

In the kitchen was a cast iron stove and scrubbed wooden table.

Taking pride of place in the sitting room was a chest of drawers.

Far away from China it had come, on a ship with Ruby's mother.

In the drawers were her most treasured possessions.

In Ruby's town there was no Autumn, Winter or Spring and Summer – but a Wet Season and a Dry Season.

The Dry season. The grass turned from green, to pink and gold and the river became a place for picnics.

The children ran and played on stretches of sand by shallow pools, and dived into sparkling waterholes.

Then there was the Wet Season. Clouds appeared in the blue sky. Moths and bugs buzzed around the lights at night. Flickers of lightning lit the inky skies.

Hotter and hotter grew the days, till thunder rumbled overhead.

The first heavy drops of rain raised dust, then down it came - a deluge.

The 'Wet': Frogs breaking out in song. Everyone glad knowing the cattle on the plain would have green grass again.

But… Keep away from the river! The river breaking its banks! Flooding the countryside with brown foaming waters all the way to the Gulf of Carpentaria, where even the boats run for shelter.

At the years end, drovers would come home.

Worn camp gear ready for repairs; horses looking for a spell.

Ruby and her friends loved listening to stories of the overlanding mobs. Stories of cattle panicked, suddenly rushing at night. Stories of favourite night horses which men trusted with their lives.

Boorooloola, Bedouri, Dajarra, and Windorah – the melodious names of little towns came as music to Ruby's ears and set her imagination soaring.

Years rolled on, and Ruby fell in love with a tall brown drover who's name was Joe.

They were married, and set off for Coronation Station to take delivery of their mob of bullocks for the journey south.

Carefully strapped into the wagonette was the Chinese chest of drawers. It was a wedding present to Ruby from her Mum and Dad.

Ruby was in charge of the cooking. Two horses, faithful Opal and fretful Spinifex were in shafts as they travelled along.

Day by day, pack up dinner camp, move onto night camp. Get the fire going, start the bread. Ruby had learned to bake crusty bread in the camp oven nested in hot ashes and coals. The wagonette always kept ahead of the mob, trudging along in the dusty haze.

Sometimes their way lay through spinifex dotted hills, sometimes out on endless plains of shimmering silver grass.

The drover, an ever-watchful eye on that brindle rogue that would slip off into the scrub, if ever it got a chance. Drover's light hand on the reins of this skittish horse, fresh from months of freedom during the wet season

Buckets of beef, Ruby's crusty bread and boiling billies greeted Joe and the other hungry riders as they came into the camp at sundown.

Night was a special time. A million stars scattered above. Pannikins of tea were passed around as they stretched their limbs and yarned over the day, over past droving trips, and more philosophical matters, before rolling out their swags.

One such night, by the light of the campfire Ruby sat stitching a small garment. She was having a baby.

From the chest of the drawers out had come her silk wedding dress, scissors and thread. She snipped and stitched.

Rosebuds were embroidered and lace whipped on.

This baby would have the best her clever hands could provide.

Full moon, morning star, sunlit days passed as the mob moved onward, until one frosty night baby was born. Bonny she was, with dark eyes and rosy cheeks.

They called her Bonnie.

The bottom drawer of the chest became her cradle. With soft mattress and patchwork rug, it was perfect size for Bonnie.

As they moved on, Bonnie listened to the lullaby of jangling harness, or was rocked to sleep by the movement of the wagonette.

But what lay up ahead?

The river channels, usually dry this time of year, were spreading across the land like a network of unravelled rope.

Nobody knew there had been big rain to the north, and nobody knew that the brown water was rushing along as never before.

The wagonette splashed and rattled across the first channels – just a trickle of debris filled water.

As she approached the main crossing Ruby noticed milk coffee-coloured water frothing against the dry creek bank. The water was rising.

A knot of fear in her stomach, she scanned the scene ahead. Water was swirling and eddying treacherously around partly submerged trees.

She examined the track up the far side. Good old Opal and Spinifex were old stagers of this stock route. Ruby knew that horses choose instinctively where to go.

With an anxious glance over the camp gear, secure in place – baby sleeping in her cradle, wedged as usual beside the tuckerbox, Ruby flapped the reins over the horses' shiny rumps and they plunged forward.

The current was strong. Then, chest deep thundering water was all that could be heard. The flood was much deeper than Ruby expected.

"Come on" Ruby whispered, sitting up straight. She could only rely on the horses. Then, they were swimming, a brown surge lapped the load, the current swept them sideways. Ruby held her breath.

Then THUD as hooves touched ground again. Oh! Suddenly Spinifex was struggling, and going down. Frightened white eyes showed as her hooves sank into a hole, invisible in the depths.

As Spinifex panicked, the wagonette tilted. Everything had been jarred and shifted. Bonnie, in her wooden cradle, was floating away, carried on that swiftly moving current.

Spinifex floundered, then found a foothold, and leaped up the bank.

The whole turnout came to a shuddering halt on dry ground. Horses trembled as water poured off everything.

Shaking, but relieved, Ruby turned to pick up her baby.

There was nothing but an empty space. Unbelieving and confused, she looked back on the water they had crossed. There was the cradle swishing along in the flood, being carried swiftly downstream.

In an instant, Ruby was back in the river, the current dragging at her clothes carrying her into the main stream in moments.

She struck out towards the cradle as rushing water splashed against her tear-streaked face.

The flood pushed her, this way and that way. A branch floated past and was tugged under by some hidden undertow. "Just keep going" Ruby desperately repeated to herself.

"Don't lose site of her".

Swimming, swimming and gasping for breath she was being swept towards a cluster of prickly bushes poking above the wash.

There the cradle was caught among the frail branches of those bushes. Ruby prayed to reach it before another surge set it free.

Ruby reached out and touched the cradle. It rocked dangerously and swung free of it's branch and began to circle – round and round in the eddy.

Just then Ruby felt something solid underfoot. That bend in the creek had a rocky outcrop on its bed, so her feet had made contact. What a relief! Grabbing a branch she caught the swirling cradle with its precious cargo, and pulled it towards the bank.

Joe and the men with the travelling mob were unaware that just days before there had been a thunderstorm at Cathedral Hills, now a hazy blue on the horizon.

The result: This torrent filling the creek channels.

It was when the lead of the mob smelt the water and quickened pace that Joe rode ahead.

He caught sight of the water, and horrified, kicked his horse into a gallop. Seeing the wagonette tracks going straight into the flood, he urged his horse and swam through the seething waters.

Up the bank, past a scattering of camp gear, he soon came upon the wagonette under a clump of coolabahs.

Opal and Spinifex were calmly feeding among trailing, tangled harness.

Where were Ruby and Bonnie?

Joe looked over the surface of water........... Nothing.

No time to be lost, he set his horse at a flying pace downstream, searching for any sign.

"How could this happen"

Thoughts race through Joe's mind. "Ruby is a good swimmer, but even a strong swimmer can be lost in a flash flood"

"Night soon, and darkness."

Desperately he pressed his tiring horse over gravel and potholes.

On the bend ahead a patch of gnarled lignum-bush straggled in the brown wash. Joe watched the water and steadied his horse.

Among the grey green bush something caught his attention.

In the speckled shade there he saw Ruby in an exhausted sleep, clinging to Bonnie.

Beside them, baby rug flung over it's side, was Bonnie's cradle, the drawer from Ruby's chest of drawers.

Mum finished her story.

"That is why this old chest of drawers is so precious, Tatum, Grandma's Precious Chest of Drawers."

As the moonlight shone through the windows, Tatum dreamed of her great-great grandmother, Ruby. The journeys she made were woven into Tatum's dreams like ribbons of silver starlight.

BRINGING UP THE TAIL

I was introduced to riding when I was three or four,
Following my Dad about and always wanting more.
Back when normal practice was to check things from a horse
To tag along when Dad rode out, was par for the course.

The distances we travelled, to a kid sometimes seemed tough,
With heat, the flies, jig-jogging, still I couldn't get enough.
Progressing then to mustering, I didn't wan't to fail,
Thought I was indispensible, bringing up the tail.

It remained like this for quite awhile, we became a team.
Promoted to better horses, the lead became my dream.
When pushing the tail along, not a lot of call for speed,
I started looking longingly at the action in the lead.

As we both grew older, of't times there came a chance,
To give back-up in the front, the signal was Dad's glance
Then with more experience, Dad eventually did concede,
His stint was on the tail while I worked up the lead.

As time moved on, the cycle was started once again,
Kids of our own, mustering, it happened just the same.
Mustering cattle on the run, through scrub, up hill, down dale,
The old man steering in the lead, kids pushing up the tail.

Then as the kids grew older, and I was getting on,
With their improved ability, my job in front is gone.
I'm now rising sixty, although I'm not so frail.
When it's hectic in the lead I'm bringing up the tail.

The cycle is completed in this wicked world of strife,
The kids are raising families bringing joy into our life.
We have a cute grand-daughter, who through life will sail,
I'm awaiting the enjoyment of helping Lacy on the tail.

Bob Marshal - *Aramac*

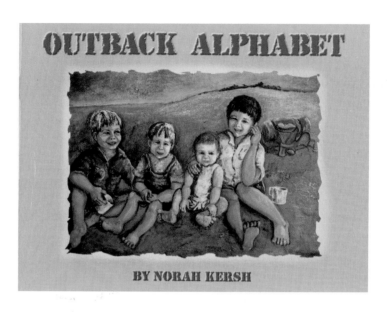

To Order this Book
Contact us at:

Boolarong
Press

35 Hamilton Road, Moorooka, Queensland 4105
Phone: (07) 3848 8200   Fax: (07) 3848 8077
e-mail: mail@boolarongpress.com.au
Visit us online: www.boolarongpress.com.au

OUTBACK COUNTOUT

BY NORAH KERSH

To Order this Book
Contact us at:

Boolarong Press

35 Hamilton Road, Moorooka, Queensland 4105
Phone: (07) 3848 8200   Fax: (07) 3848 8077
e-mail: mail@boolarongpress.com.au
Visit us online: www.boolarongpress.com.au